W9-CYW-591

THE WHISKERS SISTERS

#2 THE MYSTERY OF THE TREE STUMP GHOST

MissPATY

GRAPHIC UNIVERSE™ • MINNEAPOLIS

Story and illustrations by MissPATY
Translation by Nathan Sacks

First American edition published in 2018 by Graphic Universe™

Les Soeurs Moustaches, Tome 2: Le mystère de la vieille souche

Published by arrangement with Sylvain Coissard Agency in cooperation with Nicolas Grivel Agency

Graphic Universe™ is a trademark of Lerner Publishing Group, Inc.

Graphic Universe™
A division of Lerner Publishing Group, Inc.
241 First Avenue North
Minneapolis, MN 55401 USA

For reading levels and more information, look up this title at www.lernerbooks.com.

Main body text set in Andy Std-Regular 12/14.
Typeface provided by Monotype Typography.

Library of Congress Cataloging-in-Publication Data

The Cataloging-in-Publication Data for *The Mystery of the Tree Stump Ghost* is on file at the Library of Congress.
ISBN 978-1-5124-2528-4 (lib. bdg.)
ISBN 978-1-5415-1045-6 (pbk.)
ISBN 978-1-5124-9860-8 (eb pdf)

LC record available at https://lccn.loc.gov/2017006469

Manufactured in the United States of America
1-41274-23241-6/5/2017

Only one more letter to deliver...

I must be quick!

?
But... what is that?

ALERT! ALERT!
It's a ghost!

Oh dear! My hat!

Where's Grandpa?
We've been waiting forever.

He's the Guardian of the Forest, Maya! Remember?
...Want some popcorn?

But what if the ghost strikes again?
Ah, whatever.
Ghosts don't exist!

Forget what the animals told you.

Ta-DAA!

Of course ghosts exist, Mia!
Nope! Not possible.
They AREN'T REAL.

AAAHH!

MAY!

Wasn't even scared.
CLACK

Hello, girls!

How about a bedtime story?

A story? Oh!
Tell us about the ghost!
Yeah, the ghost!

What ghost?
Ga ga.

You know, the stump ghost!
Explain to Maya that it's not real.
Which is real.

Okay, if you insist...
but I warn you...
Ga!
Ga!

It's a little scary.

Legend says that a ghost wanders near the Old Stump...

It watches for lost travelers...
and pulls them underground!

YIKES!

HA HA
HA
HA

Come now, girls. It's just a story.
HA

Thank goodness for that!

CLick

In all my years, I've never met a ghost.

Don't worry, girls. I am the Guardian of...
Ah, I wasn't scared.
Liar!

KABOOM

PLOP
Uh, you can use the door.
Mrs. Owl, that fireplace is dangerous!
?
Guardian!
Guardian!
KNOCK
KNOCK
KNOCK
The forest looks crazy...
My word!
Ha! Slowly now!

Hello, Guardian.
Great Deer?

I'm sorry to spoil your evening...

...But this is urgent!

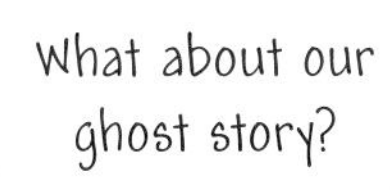
What about our ghost story?

What a mess!

Sorry, girls. I have to help.

Yes, Grandpa...

What should we do now?
I'm gonna make more popcorn.

BOOOM!

Hey, Maya—come with me to the kitchen?
I thought you never got scared!

No, I just need some help . . .

booom!

KNOCK
KNOCK
KNOCK

What if that's the ghost?

I'LL go.
'Cause ghosts DO NOT exist!

Mrs. Fox!

Good evening.
Is the Guardian of the Forest here?
Tom!

He just left.

Oh no! That's terrible!

What's going on?
Can we help?
And where's Tim?

Tim fell into a hole near the Old Stump.

We wanted to chase the ghost together.

What can we do without Grandpa?

And if the gh...

...No. NO. It's not real!
And we can't wait for Grandpa.

You're right, Mia.

Thank you.

May! Put on your jacket!
Pssh.

Ready? Let's go, Whiskers Sisters!

Here we are!
I don't like it out here.
Nobody likes it out here.
The Old Stump is haunted.

Tim!
Tim! Can you hear us?

No time to waste!

Got it!

We're good!

Hold it, May!
You stay here.

Do you see anything?
Not a thing!

May!
May!

Yippeee! May, I'm coming!

TOM!

TOM!
I'm picking up Tim's scent!

May!
You DID NOT listen, as usual.

Forget it...
She doesn't understand.
Over there!

AAAAH!
AAAAH!

Phew.
Yep. Those were bats.

We're okay. We're okay...
Let's move!

STOP!

!?

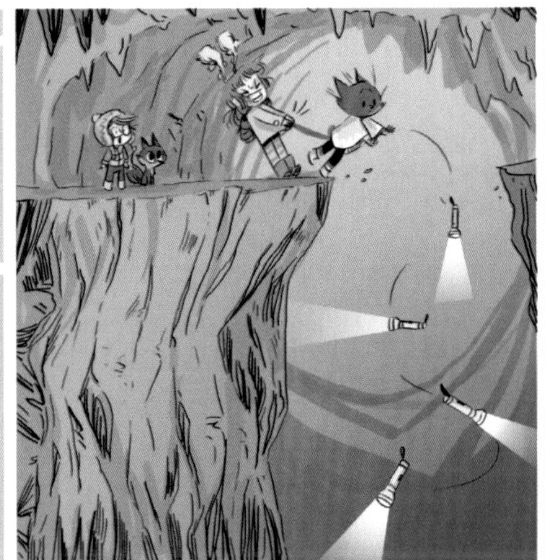

My flashlight!
Plop.

We're stuck in the dark!
Wait, I still have mine.

Ah-HA!
Let's find a way forward.

Whoo-hoo!
Careful!
Cool!

SNIFF
SNIFF
SNIFF
SNIFF

?
SNiFF
SNiFF

Wow, look!
WELCOME
SNiiiiFF
SNiFF

Ghosts have houses?
With doors and doormats?
Oh!
SNiFF
SNiFF

Tim?
SNiFF
SNiFF

THE GHOST!

Meanwhile, in the field...
Here we are!
?

But who did this?

We have no idea!
Help...
A little help, Guardian?

Move, my friends! Push!
Push!
I'm nearly out!

Thanks!
I was a little stuck.

What we need is a plan.

Who's been digging these holes?
No idea.

It was the ghost! Saw it with my own two eyes.
He stole my hat.

Let's form two groups.
One to clean up the field...

...And one to investigate this mystery.

Who will volunteer?
Me.
I want my hat back.
Next time?

Very good, Mrs. Owl. You'll team up with me.
Anyone else?

Who wants to meet a GHOST?
We're not crazy!

Guardian! We found something!
This way!

Acorns and wild strawberries? Is this a trail?
Strange. Why would a ghost do that?
Let's follow it and flush out the ghost!
Squirrels, you come with us.
Great Deer, can you and the others refill these holes?
I'll take care of it, Guardian.

Let's see what this mystery is really about.
Onward!

The ghost!
It's not possible!

He won't get away, Maya!
The rope!

The rope?
Yes, that's it!

Remember our motto! "You never fail if you keep trying!"
Yeah!

HA HA HA HA HA HA HA

Charge!

STOP!
Don't hurt him!

Tim!
TIM!?

Tim.
There you are!
Tom!
May!

This isn't a ghost.
It's Mr. Hermit!
He helped me out.

Howdy!

He's human?

Welcome.
I've never seen this guy anywhere in the forest.

We are so happy to have visitors!

We invite you to drink some tea!
"We"? It's just him.
Are you sure it's okay to follow this guy, Tim?
Yeah, he's real nice.
And his tea is great!
He seems a little unusual, right?
Let's find out!
Welcome to our home! Please, sit!

Very pretty.
We're right under the Old Stump!
You can tell us some news...

...While we have treats and tea!

So what brings you down here?
We followed Tim.
We were very worried.

This is good!
What is it?

Nettle tea...
...With bug juice!

Ughh!

What do you mean by "we"?

We!
Me, the trees,
the leaves, my stick collection.
HA HA HA HA HA HA HA HA HA
Get it?

Um... yes?
May, don't drink that.
But it's good!

Don't you feel lonely down here?

You've got to see things a different way, young lady!
We're never alone!

This way!

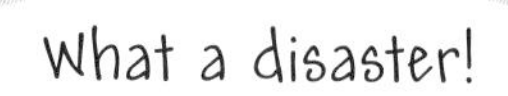

Hey! Scram!

What a disaster!
They ate the whole trail!

Quiet!
Somebody's coming!

The ghost who stole my hat!

Hold on, look!
It's Mrs. Fox.

Guardian!
Finally.
Psst.
Psst.
Hey!

Over there!
Let's go!

They've found the rest of the trail.
Guardian, I...

Oh, my.
A cave?

By the hairs of my beard...
...Look at all this stuff!
The plot thickens.

But what is THAT?

ALERT! ALERT! My hat!

Give it back!

What were those creatures?

?

Thieves!

WHAM!

Mrs. Owl!
You all right?

Super!
Everything is fine.

Whoops!

Where are you from?
Oh, just beyond the forest.

I was picking wild strawberries one day.
They are the best!

And bam!
I fell down here.

And after that?
?

Didn't you see my little buddies?

See who?
Let's get out of here. Fast.
POK

?
?

?
BOOM

Grandpa?
Ga!
Ga!
Mommy!

Girls!?
Tim!
Tom!
MY HAT!

We fell through a hole...
...But where are we?
Inside the Old Stump.

My little ones! Come here!

They call me Mr. Hermit. These are my little companions.

They're wood sprites!

Oh! They are so cute!

You're not scared?

They're very shy.

Thanks for your hospitality!
But don't touch my hat.

I don't have much...
It's an original recipe.
But please enjoy some tea.

Don't drink it, Grandpa!

Tell us your story!
Yeah!
We're listening!
You mean, how I got my stick collection?

No, no!
Okay!
Tell us about the wood sprites!
Though it's a beautiful collection.
Ga, gaa!
But if you insist...
The history of the wood sprites begins here...

In the heart of the forest stood a sacred oak tree.

It was ageless. Older than the forest's oldest animal. It had always been there.

For all the animals, the tree was the heart of forest life. Under the shade of its branches, they enjoyed peace and harmony.

And a group of special little creatures watched over it: the wood sprites.

But one day, a storm broke out. A thunderbolt struck the tree in half. The tree caught fire, and the animals fled. The only thing that remained was a charred stump.

The sprites were orphans now. They burrowed deep into the dead tree's roots. Sad and lonely, they began to forget their role as the tree's protectors.

Until I accidentally fell into the cave underneath the Old Stump. They helped me, healed me, and started looking after me.

Together, we're a family . . .

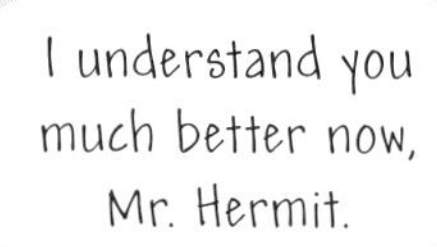

I understand you much better now, Mr. Hermit.
But one thing confuses me.

Why were you digging holes in the big field?
It looked quite messy.
You scared us!

My bad! We needed more bugs for our tea!

We're sorry about that.
We'll repair the damage.

Oh, hey—did I mention my stick collection?

Um . . .
Not again.
You did! Bye now!
I use them as batons!

Now let's dance, sprites!
1, 2, 3 . . . boogie!
Hi
Hi
Hi
Hi
Hi
Hi

. . . We should leave him alone.

You are always welcome in our home!
I'll try the tea next time!
Pleasure to meet you!
Oh, my. The sun has set already!
See ya!
Bye!
Thanks for your help!

Duty calls! I still have mail to deliver.
Good night, Mrs. Owl.
See ya!
Good-bye!

That was so much fun!
What a story!
I wasn't even scared.
The Great Deer will never believe us!

Hey, Maya! We can write about this in our notebook of adventures.
Yes! I'll do the drawings.

It's already bedtime, girls. You'll have to wait until tomorrow morning.
Bed?
Huh?

Can't you tell us a story?
Yeah! Yeah!
I don't think so, girls.
You must be exhausted!
Gaa?

Us?
Never!

It is time to go to bed.
We aren't tired!
No no.

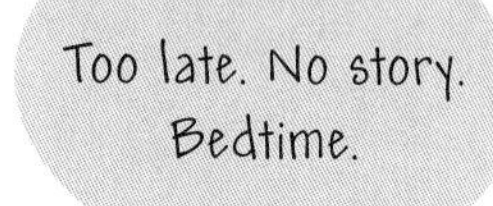
Too late. No story. Bedtime.

Up you go!
So unfair.

Sweet dreams!
Good night, Grandpa!
Zzz

Good night, girls!

Today we made
new friends:
Mr. Hermit
and the Wood
Sprites!
MIA